SCOOBY-DOO!
DISAPPEARING DONUTS

By Gail Herman

Illustrated by Duendes del Sur

SCHOLASTIC INC.
New York   Toronto   London   Auckland   Sydney
Mexico City   New Delhi   Hong Kong

ISBN 0-439-16168-1

20 19 18   5 6/0

Designed by Mary Hall
Printed in the U.S.A.
First Scholastic printing, April 2000

"Rummy!"
Scooby-Doo rubbed his tummy
and looked inside the donut
store.
His friends looked too.
"Doodles Donuts!" Shaggy read
the sign.
"Let's go inside!"

DOODLES
DONUTS

"Hi! I'm Dora," said the owner.

"Hello," said Fred. "I'm Fred and these are my friends, Daphne, Velma, Shaggy, and Scooby-Doo."

"We would like some donuts," said Shaggy.
"Rummy!" Scooby-Doo said. In a flash,
Shaggy and Scooby-Doo gobbled down
dozens of donuts.

Velma and Daphne laughed.

"Hey, leave some for us," Fred joked.

"Your dog sure loves donuts," Dora
said. "Just like my doggie, Doodles."
"I guess that's why you call the shop
Doodles Donuts," Velma said.

A few days later, the gang came
back for more donuts.
But the shop looked different.
Dora was packing everything up!

She was closing Doodles Donuts! "I have a big problem," she told the gang. "Donuts have been disappearing."

Dora sighed. "Every night I put the donuts in a bin in the back room. And in the morning, the donuts are gone! Last night, I stayed late," Dora

said. "And I spotted a huge, scary creature covered with fur. It was digging around in the bin . . . eating my donuts!"

"A ronster?" Scooby asked.

"How can I stay open?" Dora asked. "The monster will come back. And who knows what could happen?"

Velma stepped forward.

"We'll help," Velma told Dora.

"We'll stay at the donut shop tonight," Fred said.

"We'll find out the truth about this monster," Daphne added.

"Stay in the shop tonight?" Shaggy shook his head.

"Ro way!" Scooby added.

"That goes double fudge donuts for me!" said Shaggy.

"Please stay," Dora begged. "You can have all
the free donuts you can eat."
"Rokay!" Scooby agreed.
"That goes triple chocolate donuts for me!"
said Shaggy.

That night, the gang stayed in the shop.
Scooby and Shaggy slurped down donut
after donut.
Finally Shaggy yawned. He was tired from
eating.

"We might as well hide now, good buddy," he
told Scooby. They closed their eyes to nap.
ROAR! A loud shriek woke them up!

Zoinks! It was awful!

"It's coming from the back room!" Velma said.

"Like, Scoob and I will explore the front,"
  Shaggy said.

Velma, Fred, and Daphne raced to the back room. Scooby and Shaggy slipped out the front.

It was dark. Shaggy could barely see.

"Scooby?" he whispered.

But Scooby was gone!

Shaggy had to find the rest of the gang.

He had to tell them Scooby had disappeared.

Shaggy gulped. He tiptoed around the
side of the building.
All at once a giant, furry monster leaped
out.

DOODLES
DONUTS

"Monster!" Shaggy shouted. Somewhere he
heard Scooby shout, "Ronster!"
The gang rushed over.
Velma turned on her flashlight.

Shaggy gazed at the big, furry creature.
Scooby gazed at the big, furry creature.
"Scooby?" said Shaggy.
"Raggy?" said Scooby.

"You each thought the other was the
monster," Fred explained.
"It was so dark, you couldn't see," Daphne
said.

"And that gives me an idea!" Velma exclaimed. "Come on! I know who the real monster is!"
She led the others out back.

"ROAR!" The shriek grew louder.
Then they saw it.
The monster.

Huge.

Furry.

Scary.

Velma switched on the floodlights.

"Roodles!" said Scooby.

"You're right," said Shaggy.

"It's Dora's dog, Doodles!" Daphne said.

The monster wasn't big or scary at all.

"What's going on?" asked Dora.
She had just come by to check on the gang.
"Doodles is the monster," Velma explained.

"The moonlight and shadows just made her look like a monster," Fred added.

"Good job!" said Dora. "Now I can keep my shop open. How can I thank you?"

The gang grinned. Scooby rubbed
his tummy.

"Keep making those donuts," Fred said.

"And we can keep eating donuts!" said Shaggy.

"Scooby-Dooby-Doo!" Scooby barked.